My Heart Is a Magic House

WRITTEN BY **Julie Jacobs**

ILLUSTRATED BY **Bernadette Pons**

ALBERT WHITMAN & COMPANY, MORTON GROVE, ILLINOIS

15.95

E
FICTION
JAC

Library of Congress Cataloging-in-Publication Data

Jacobs, Julie.
My heart is a magic house / by Julie Jacobs ; illustrated by Bernadette Pons.
written p. cm. ump, i#bill.
Summary: A mother explains that when the new baby arrives, her heart will add a room
so everyone will always receive the same amount of love.
ISBN 13: 978-0-8075-5335-0 (hardcover)
[1. Babies—Fiction. 2. Love—Fiction. 3. Mother and child—Fiction.]
I. Pons, Bernadette, ill. II. Title.
PZ7.J152437Myh 2007 [E]—dc22 2006023399

The design is by Carol Gildar.

For more information about Albert Whitman & Company,
please visit our web site at www.albertwhitman.com.

For my two brothers, Ian and Greg. The rooms in my heart for you—and for your new families—get bigger every year.—J.J.

To Emma, Marion, and Louise.—B.P.

"Where will the new baby sleep, Mommy?"

"Next to Daddy and me in a bassinet, Stephanie," Mommy said. "Later the baby will share your room."

"But it's *my* room! I don't want to share it."

"You'll sleep in your new big bed, and the baby will be in your old crib. There will always be enough room for you."

"Will the baby play with my toys? The blocks and trucks are okay, but not Rosie! She's mine!"

"The baby will get some new toys and
share some of yours. But Rosie is just for you."

"What will the new baby eat? *My* food?"

"The baby will eat special foods for a long time. There will always be enough for you to eat."

"But will you still love me, Mommy?"

"Oh, Stephanie, I will never run out of love for you! I will love you forever and ever, as big as the sky and the ocean and the whole wide world!

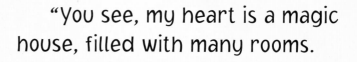

"You see, my heart is a magic house, filled with many rooms.

"When I was a little girl, there were rooms for my mommy and daddy, my brothers and sister, and my dog, Herman.

Herman

My brother

My mommy

My sister

My daddy

Your daddy

My brother

Buster

"After I met your
daddy, my heart grew
a special room for him.
But there was still plenty
of room for everyone.

"Then we got Buster,
and of course he has
his own room, too.

"And then I added another room when you were a baby. I love you so much, and I always will!

"When the baby is born, there will be another room in my heart. But the room for you will be just as big as it is now."

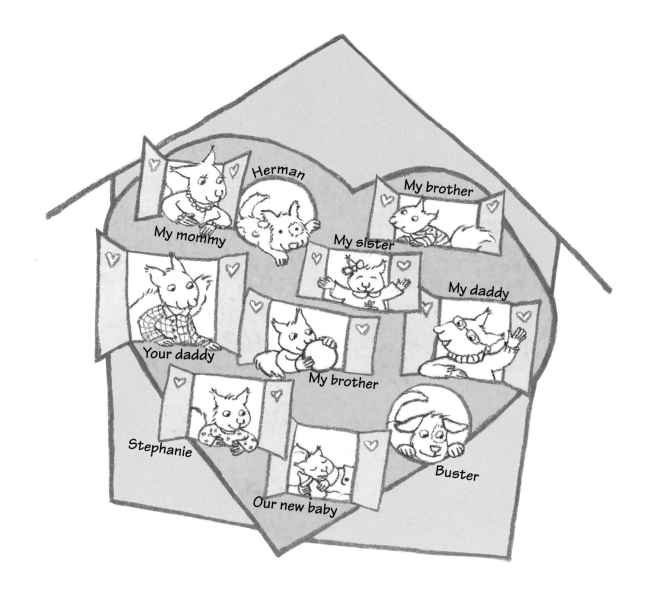

My mommy

Herman

My brother

My sister

Your daddy

My brother

My daddy

Stephanie

Our new baby

Buster

"Can I add a room in my heart for the baby, too?"

"Oh, yes," Mommy said.

"And Mommy, the baby
can even hold Rosie."